To

From

Date

Quinn's Promise Rock

WRITTEN BY

CHRISTIE THOMAS

ILLUSTRATED BY

SYDNEY HANSON

Quinn was a thoughtful little owl who always had a lot of questions.

One night, Quinn and her father went flying together.
As they soared through the forest, searching for some
dinner, Quinn had a sudden, scary thought.

"Daddy?" she asked.
"Yes, my little owl?"

"What if I get lost? What if you dive and I don't notice? What if you get too far ahead of me and I can't find you? You fly so quietly, what if—"

"Quinn."

Quinn's father was smiling. He turned away slowly and started flying toward a mountain. Quinn followed him. Why wasn't her father saying anything?

Quinn flapped her wings harder as they flew up, up, up, and she started to breathe heavier. Where were they going?

Her father circled around a huge stone on top of the mountain and then perched on it. Quinn landed and puffed hard as she tried to catch her breath.

"Daddy," she panted, "why did we come way up here?"

Her father lifted his wing and pointed toward the

"Do you see that tree way down there?" he asked.

Quinn nodded.

"Do you recognize it?"

Quinn's bright owl eyes looked keenly at the tree, and then she blurted, "That's OUR tree! That's where our nest is!"

Her father nodded and said, "This mountain will always be here. It never moves. And it will always show you the way to get home."

"Quinn, God is like
this rocky mountain.
God is always here,
he never changes,
and he will never
leave. He will show
you the way you
should go."

Quinn nodded thoughtfully. Suddenly, she felt a drop on her beak...and then another drop on her head. Her father spread his wings and started flying back down the mountain. Quinn followed.

The rain started to come down faster, and the wind came in gusts.

It pushed Quinn's little owl body this way and that, and she became frightened.

Cold water poured off her feathers, and she could barely see her father through the raindrops.

Her father slowed down and then landed inside a tiny cave on the side of the mountain. Quinn landed beside him and shook the water off her feathers.

Her father lifted a wing, and Quinn snuggled underneath it to warm up.

As the storm roared on, her father hugged her close and said, "This cave is a safe place. It protects us from the wind and rain."

"Quinn, God is like this rocky cave. God can protect you during the scariest times in life. When you feel afraid, he is right there, just like this cave, and you can take shelter in him."

Eventually the storm stopped and the sky cleared.
The stars came out, and Quinn and her father
started off again under the shining moon.

They flew silently through the night, sometimes swooping down to eat but mostly just flying side by side.

Just as Quinn was starting to get quite tired, her father dove toward the ground and landed right on the forest floor. Quinn landed beside him and looked up at him with wide, wondering eyes.

Quinn's father picked up a little rock with his talon and gave it to her.

Then he looked into Quinn's eyes and said, "If you tuck this rock into your feathers, you can carry it everywhere you go. You will feel it, hard against your body."

"Quinn, God is like this tiny rock. Even though he is big like a mountain and safe like a cave, you can also carry him everywhere you go. God is always with you."

Quinn's eyes grew even bigger.

"So if I get lost or scared, I can feel my little rock and remember that God is with me!"

"That's right, my thoughtful little owl. God will show you the way you should go, he will be a safe place, and he will always be with you."

The sun began to rise, and Quinn tucked the little rock into a safe place in her feathers. As she and her father flew home, she could hardly wait to tell her mama about this strange and wonderful night.

Best of all, she would show her the little promise rock.

Did You Know...

Owls are the quietest fliers because of the special feathers God gave them. This enables them to swoop down and capture prey without being noticed. That is why Quinn was so worried about losing her father!

A Note to Parents

Most young children sometimes feel separation anxiety. As caregivers, we can reassure them that we will always come back for them. But the reality is that no one can truthfully make that promise except God. God is the only one who will always love our children, always guide their path, always provide refuge, and always be at their side.

Making such an abstract concept real to children is difficult...which is where *Quinn's Promise Rock* comes in! Help your children find a small rock—small enough to keep in a pocket—and give it to them after reading *Quinn's Promise Rock*. Remind your children that whenever they feel scared, they can put their hand in their pocket and be reminded that God is with them and will help them.

Here are some child-friendly verses you can teach your children.

Don't worry about anything; instead, pray about everything. Tell God what you need, and thank him for all he has done. Then you will experience God's peace, which exceeds anything we can understand. His peace will guard your hearts and minds as you live in Christ Jesus (Philippians 4:6-7).

Be strong and courageous! Do not be afraid or discouraged. For the LORD your God is with you wherever you go (Joshua 1:9).

How good it is to be near God! I have made the Sovereign LORD my shelter (Psalm 73:28).

I am with you always, even to the end of the age (Matthew 28:20).

Christie Thomas, the "Bedtime Devo Mama," has written for various websites, including The MOB Society and The Better Mom. She's the author of the interactive and multisensory devotional book *Wise for Salvation*. Christie lives in Alberta, Canada, with her husband and three boys.

Sydney Hanson was raised in Minnesota alongside numerous pets and brothers. Her illustrations and paintings still reflect these early adventures and are marked by a love for animals and the natural world. Sydney has worked for several major animation shops, including Nickelodeon and Disney Interactive.

Cover design by Connie Gabbert Design + Illustration

Interior design by Left Coast Design

Published in association with the literary agency of Credo Communications, LLC, Grand Rapids, Michigan, www.credocommunications.net.

HARVEST KIDS is a registered trademark of The Hawkins Children's LLC. Harvest House Publishers, Inc., is the exclusive licensee of the federally registered trademark HARVEST KIDS.

Quinn's Promise Rock

Text copyright © 2019 by Christina Thomas
Artwork copyright © 2019 by Sydney Hanson

Published by Harvest House Publishers
Eugene, Oregon 97408
www.harvesthousepublishers.com

ISBN 978-0-7369-7432-5 (hardcover)

Library of Congress Cataloging-in-Publication Data

Names: Thomas, Christie, author. | Hanson, Sydney, illustrator.
Title: Quinn's promise rock / Christie Thomas; artwork by Sydney Hanson.
Description: Eugene, Oregon: Harvest House Publishers, [2018] | Summary: Quinn, a thoughtful young owl, is reassured by her father that God is always with her, taking care of her, and he gives her a small rock to carry as a reminder. Includes science note and parent page.
Identifiers: LCCN 2018013034 (print) | LCCN 2018019079 (ebook) | ISBN 9780736974332 (ebook) ISBN 9780736974325 (hardcover)
Subjects: | CYAC: Presence of God—Fiction. | Separation anxiety—Fiction. | Owls—Fiction. Animals—Infancy—Fiction. | Father and child—Fiction.
Classification: LCC PZ7.1.T4484 (ebook) | LCC PZ7.1.T4484 Qui 2018 (print) | DDC [E]—dc23 LC record available at https://lccn.loc.gov/2018013034

Printed in China

18 19 20 21 22 23 24 25 26 / LP / 10 9 8 7 6 5 4 3 2 1